FIVE Little MONKEYS
Storybook Treasury

Eileen Christelow

Clarion Books
Houghton Mifflin Harcourt
Boston   New York

Clarion Books is an imprint of Houghton Mifflin Harcourt Publishing Company.

ISBN: 978-0-547-23873-9

Printed in Malaysia

TWP 10 9 8 7 6 5 4 3 2 1

Contents

The mama called the doctor. The doctor said,

**FIVE LITTLE MONKEYS JUMPING ON THE BED . . .
AND INTO PRINT!**

I grew up with books. As a preschooler, a favorite time of day was when my parents would come home from work, relax on the couch, and read picture books to me. At an early age, I realized the necessity of learning to read when, as a punishment for accidentally locking my parents out of their bedroom, I had to go without story-time for a week! It was agony! Worse than a spanking! After that I often dreamed I could read all by myself: picture books, entire newspapers, my father's mysteries . . . but always when I woke up, I still could not unlock the code of reading. Despite this setback, I became a full-fledged bookworm at an early age.

I continued the story-time tradition with my own daughter, Heather. We went to the library once or twice a week. We read before naptime and bedtime and times in between. What an education for a graphic designer/illustrator/photographer like myself who was hoping to learn the craft of creating picture books!

Heather introduced me to two Five Little Monkey rhymes when she was in preschool: *"Five little monkeys jumping on the bed . . ."* and *"Five little monkeys sitting in a tree, teasing Mr. Crocodile . . ."* I immediately thought they were wonderful material for a picture book, but since I was working on other stories, I tucked them away for a future project.

My first book, *Henry and the Red Stripes*, was published in 1982. My daughter was nine. Five years and several books later, I pulled out the monkey rhymes and tackled the problem of transforming them into 32-page picture books. As I drew and made dummies for the "jumping on the bed" rhyme, the monkeys took on a life of their own.

"NO MORE MONKEYS JUMPING ON THE BED!"

I read one of my dummies to a kindergarten class. I was astonished! The kids took over "reading" the book (they knew the rhyme); all I had to do was turn the pages. And the surprise ending was a big hit! That day the monkeys made their debut and it boded well for their enthusiastic acceptance by children around the world.

Five Little Monkeys Jumping on the Bed was published a year later, in 1989, and met with instant success. Children loved the monkeys' antics! The book received critical success as well. *Booklist* described the book as "pure silliness—just the kind kids like." The monkeys were a hit. *Five Little Monkeys Sitting in a Tree* followed a few years later.

Many books—*Letters from a Desperate Dog*, *VOTE!*, *Where's the Big Bad Wolf?*, *The Great Pig Search*—and many years later, the little monkeys and their harried mama continue to insert themselves into my work: I might start a project with one character in mind and before I know it the five little monkeys and their lively antics have taken over. The result? To date there are seven books about the five little monkeys, the first five of which appear in this treasury.

I should also give credit for some of these stories to the schoolchildren I've visited with around the country. My program at schools always includes a group effort at developing a story. I draw while the kids come up with ideas—often about the monkeys. *Five Little Monkeys Wash the Car* and *Five Little Monkeys with Nothing to Do* were inspired by requests for a story about monkeys and cars. I know: *Five Little Monkeys with Nothing to Do* isn't about a car! But over the years I've found my stories develop in the most circuitous ways.

—Eileen Christelow

FIVE Little MONKEYS
jumping on the bed

It was bedtime. So five little monkeys took a bath.

Five little monkeys put on their pajamas.

Five little monkeys brushed their teeth.

Five little monkeys said good night to their mama.

Then...five little monkeys jumped on the bed!

One fell off and bumped his head.

The mama called the doctor. The doctor said,

"No more monkeys jumping on the bed!"

22

So four little monkeys...

...jumped on the bed.

One fell off and bumped his head.

The mama called the doctor.

The doctor said,

"No more monkeys jumping on the bed!"

So three little monkeys jumped on the bed.

One fell off and bumped her head.

The mama called the doctor.

The doctor said,

"No more monkeys jumping on the bed!"

So two little monkeys jumped on the bed.

One fell off and bumped his head.

The mama called the doctor.

The doctor said,

"No more monkeys jumping on the bed!"

So one little monkey jumped on the bed.

She fell off and bumped her head.

The mama called the doctor.

The doctor said,

"NO MORE MONKEYS JUMPING ON THE BED!"

So five little monkeys fell fast asleep.

"Thank goodness!" said the mama.

"Now I can go to bed!"

FIVE Little MONKEYS
sitting in a tree

Five little monkeys and their mama
walk down to the river for a picnic supper.

Mama spreads out a blanket
and settles down for a snooze . . .

. . . while five little monkeys
climb a tree to watch Mr. Crocodile.

Five little monkeys, sitting in a tree,
tease Mr. Crocodile, "Can't catch me!"

Along comes Mr. Crocodile . . .

SNAP!

Oh, no! Where is she?

Four little monkeys, sitting in a tree,
tease Mr. Crocodile, "Can't catch me!"
Along comes Mr. Crocodile . . .

Oh, no! Where is he?

Three little monkeys, sitting in a tree,
tease Mr. Crocodile, "Can't catch me!"
Along comes Mr. Crocodile . . .

Oh, no! Where is he?

Two little monkeys, sitting in a tree,
tease Mr. Crocodile, "Can't catch me!"
Along comes Mr. Crocodile . . .

Oh, no! Where is she?

Now there's only one little
monkey, sitting in the tree,
teasing Mr. Crocodile,
"Can't catch me!"
Along comes Mr. Crocodile . . .

66

Oh, no! There are no little monkeys sitting in the tree. But, wait! Look!

1 2 3 4 5

Five little monkeys, sitting in the tree!

Their mama hugs them.

Their mama scolds them.
"Never tease a crocodile.
It's not nice—and it's dangerous."

Then five little monkeys and their mama
eat a delicious picnic supper.

And they do not tease Mr. Crocodile again!

FIVE Little MONKEYS
with nothing to do

It is summer. There is no school.
Five little monkeys tell their mama,
"We're bored. There is nothing to do!"
   "Oh yes there is," says Mama.
"Grandma Bessie is coming for lunch,
and the house must be neat and clean.

"So . . . you can pick up your room."

Five little monkeys pick up and pick up and pick up . . .

. . . until everything is put away.

"Good job!" says Mama.
"But we're bored again,"
say five little monkeys.
"There is nothing to do!"
"Oh yes there is," says Mama.
"You can scrub the bathroom.
The house must be neat and clean
for Grandma Bessie."

So five little monkeys scrub and scrub and scrub until the bathroom shines.

"Good job!" says Mama.
"But we're bored again,"
say five little monkeys.
"There is nothing to do!"
"Oh yes there is," says Mama.
"You can beat the dirt out of these rugs.
The house must be neat and clean
for Grandma Bessie."

Five little monkeys beat and beat and beat the rugs until there is not a speck of dirt left.

"Good job!" says Mama.
"But we're bored again," say five little monkeys.
"There is nothing to do!"

"Oh yes there is," says Mama.
"You can pick some berries down by the swamp.
Grandma Bessie loves berries for dessert."

Five little monkeys run down
to the muddy, muddy swamp.

They pick and pick and pick berries
until Mama calls, "It's time to come home!"

Five little monkeys run inside
while Mama picks flowers.

"Put the berries in the kitchen,"
calls Mama. "Wash your faces
and put on clean clothes."

Five little monkeys wash their faces . . .

. . . and they put on clean clothes.
"Grandma Bessie is here!" calls Mama.

Five little monkeys race outside.

They hug and kiss Grandma Bessie.

"We've been busy all day!" they say.

"We cleaned the house and picked berries just for you!"

"I love berries," says Grandma Bessie. "And I love a clean house, too!"

They all go inside.

"Oh my!" says Grandma Bessie.
"Oh dear!" says Mama.
"Oh no!" say five little monkeys.
"Who messed up our nice, clean house?"

"I can't imagine," says Mama.
"But whoever did has plenty to do!"

FIVE Little MONKEYS
bake a birthday cake

Five little monkeys wake up with the sun.
"Today is Mama's birthday!"

Five little monkeys tiptoe past Mama sleeping.
"Let's bake a birthday cake!"

"Sh-h-h! Don't wake up Mama!"

One little monkey reads the recipe.
"Two cups of flour. Three teaspoons of baking powder.

"Sift everything together.
But don't sneeze! You'll wake up Mama!"

"Sh-h-h! Don't wake up Mama!"

Five little monkeys check on Mama.

"She's still asleep. We can finish making the cake."

One little monkey reads the recipe.
"Add four eggs."
Four little monkeys each get some eggs.

"And we need sugar and oil."
"Don't spill the oil!"

But one little monkey spills…

...And another little monkey slips and falls.
"Sh-h-h! Don't wake up Mama!"

Five little monkeys check on Mama.
"She's still asleep.
We can finish making the cake."

One little monkey reads the recipe.
"Next, mix everything together and put it into pans.
Then bake the cake in the oven."

Another little monkey says, "Now we can go up
to our room and make a present for Mama."

Five little monkeys start to make a present.

"Sh-h-h! Don't wake up Mama!"

One little monkey says, "Do you smell something burning?"

Five little monkeys race past Mama sleeping.
"Sh-h-h! Don't wake up Mama!"

"Oh no! The cake dripped all over."
"Turn off the oven!"
"Save the cake!"
"Sh-h-h! Don't wake up Mama!"

133

"Look! Here comes the fire engine!"
says one little monkey.
"Sh-h-h! Don't wake up Mama!"
says another little monkey.

"Where's the fire?"
shouts a fireman.
"It's not a fire!"
sniffs one little monkey.
"We ruined Mama's
birthday cake."

"Wait!" says another little monkey.
"This cake doesn't taste TOO bad."
"Frosting might help," says the
other fireman.

Five little monkeys and two firemen frost the cake.

"Now we can wake up Mama!"

Five little monkeys and two firemen
sing to Mama very, VERY, VERY LOUDLY.

And Mama wakes up!

"What a wonderful surprise," she says. "But my birthday is tomorrow!"

"Oh no!" say five little monkeys. "But can we still have birthday cake for breakfast?"

"Why not?" says Mama.

Five little monkeys, two firemen, and Mama think the birthday cake is delicious.

One little monkey whispers, "We can bake another cake tomorrow."

Another little monkey says, "Sh-h-h! Don't tell Mama!"

FIVE Little MONKEYS
wash the car

The five little monkeys,
and Mama, can never drive far
in their rickety, rattletrap
wreck of a car.

"I've had it!" says Mama.
"Let's sell this old heap!"
She makes a big sign that says,
CAR FOR SALE—CHEAP!

Then Mama goes in.
"There's some work I
should do."
"Okay," say the monkeys.
"We have work too!"

"This car is so *icky!*"
"So sticky and slimy!"
"How can we sell
an old car that's so grimy?"

"I KNOW!" says one little monkey.

So two little monkeys
spray with a hose,
while three little monkeys
scrub the car till it glows.

"But the car is still rusty!"
"It stinks! Oh, *pee-yew!*"
"No one will buy it."
"What can we do?"

"I KNOW!" says one little monkey.

I KNOW!

Then four little monkeys
find paint in the shed.
Blue, yellow, and green,
purple, pink, and bright red.

They paint the old car
with designs all around,
while one little monkey
sprays perfume he found.

The five little monkeys
sit down and wait.
But no one comes by—
and it's getting late!

I KNOW!

"The car looks terrific!"
"It smells so good too!"
"Maybe no one can see it here."
"What should we do?"

"I KNOW!" says one little monkey.

So three little monkeys
start pushing the car.
The monkey who's steering
can't see very far.

Then one little monkey
shouts, "Park it right here!
Wait! It's rolling too fast!
Can't you stop? Can't you steer?"

The monkey who's steering
can't reach the brake.
The car rolls downhill to the . . .

. . . BROWN SWAMPY LAKE!

"Well, now we're in trouble!"
"We're stuck in this goo!"
"We'll never get out."
"Oh, what can we do?"

"WE KNOW!" rumbles a voice from the swamp.

"The **CROCODILES!**"
five little monkeys all shout.
One crocodile says,
"*We'll* help you get out!"

More crocodiles rise
from the wet swampy goo.
"We'll push this old car.
But YOU must push too."

I KNOW!

The monkeys all quake.
"What they say isn't true!"
"They'll eat us for supper!"
"Oh, what can we do?"

"I KNOW!" says one little monkey.

"Oh, crocodiles!" she calls,
"I heard you were strong!
But if you need *our* help,
I must have heard wrong."

"We're strong!" roar the crocs.
"We're the strongest by far!
And we can push anything
—even a car!"

So they puff and they pant
till they look very ill.
But they push that old car
to the top of the hill.

Then one monkey whispers,
"We're *still* in a stew!
If they don't go home now,
what can we do?"

"I KNOW!" says one little monkey.

"Poor crocs!" say the monkeys.
"How tired you are!
You'll never walk home!
What you need is a . . .

...CAR!"

The crocodiles buy it.
They pay with a check,
then climb right inside.
"We can use this old wreck!"

The monkeys all run
to tell Mama their tale.
"You might have been eaten!"
(She's turning quite pale.)

"We know!" say the monkeys.
"We're lucky, it's true.
But we *did* sell the car . . .
Can we buy one that's new?"

The five little monkeys
and Mama go shop
for a fancy new car—
with a convertible top!

And the crocodiles?
They really like their old heap.
It's such a fine car
for a long summer's . . .

...SLEEP!

Learn How To Draw a Monkey!

Follow these steps and draw your very own monkey:

1 First draw a circle with two dots.

2 Add two big eyes.

3 This monkey needs fur.

4 And two ears!

5 And what about a mouth? Is he happy?

6 Or is your monkey sad?

7 And don't forget the eyebrows! They show how your monkey feels, too.

8 Here are some silly monkeys making funny faces. Look at their eyes, mouths, and eyebrows.

9 Here are some more monkeys. Trace them. Can you give them silly faces?

10 Draw the rest of the monkey.

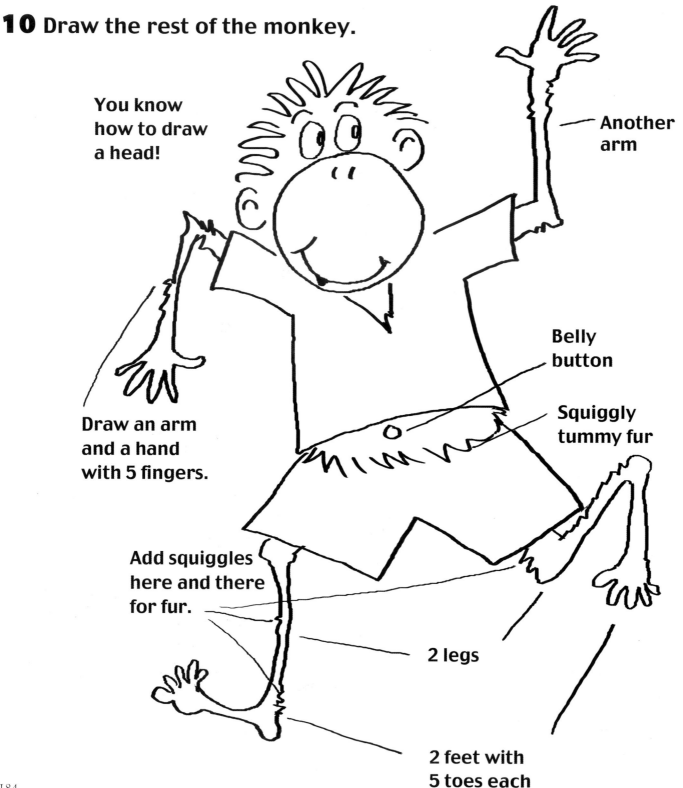

You know how to draw a head!

Another arm

Draw an arm and a hand with 5 fingers.

Belly button

Squiggly tummy fur

Add squiggles here and there for fur.

2 legs

2 feet with 5 toes each

Here are a few
monkey line drawings
you can use as
reference:

Eileen Christelow

Eileen Christelow was born in Washington, D.C., and grew up in a family of avid readers. It was in high school that she first made the leap from reader to writer, publishing her first stories in her high school's magazine.

After studying art history and drawing in college, she discovered a love of photography and began building a career as a photographer. Her interest in children's books was always strong, and after the birth of her daughter, she began thinking about writing one of her own. Her first book, *Henry and the Red Stripes,* was published in 1982.

Since then, she has written and illustrated numerous best-selling picture books including seven popular books about the Five Little Monkeys, *Letters from a Desperate Dog,* and *VOTE!*. She lives with her husband in Dummerston, Vermont, and you can learn more about her life and work on her website, www.christelow.com.

Five Little Monkeys Jumping On the Bed

Traditional

Sprightly!

Five lit - tle mon - keys jump-ing on the bed

One fell off and bumped his head

Mam - ma called the doc - tor and the doc - tor said:

"No more mon - keys jump - ing on the bed!"

FIVE Little MONKEYS

Five little monkeys jumping on the bed
One fell off and bumped his head
Mama called the doctor and the doctor said
No more monkeys jumping on the bed!

Four little monkeys jumping on the bed
One fell off and bumped his head
Mama called the doctor and the doctor said
No more monkeys jumping on the bed!

Three little monkeys jumping on the bed
One fell off and bumped his head
Mama called the doctor and the doctor said
No more monkeys jumping on the bed!

Two little monkeys jumping on the bed
One fell off and bumped his head
Mama called the doctor and the doctor said
No more monkeys jumping on the bed!

One little monkey jumping on the bed
He fell off and bumped his head
Mama called the doctor and the doctor said
No more monkeys jumping on the bed!

A little tip for parents: as you sing this song to your children, hand motions or finger puppets go a long way towards bringing this rhyme to life. Count down with your fingers, making them jump like little monkeys for the beginning of each verse. Pretend to talk on the phone when Mama calls the doctor, and wag your index finger in a mock reprimand for the refrain. Or make up your own pantomimes. Above all, feel free to be silly and have fun!